DIGGING FOR DINOSAURS

One of the most enjoyable parts of Sylvia's and my work is digging for dinosaur fossils. This is always exciting. Of course, there is a great deal of hard work. But it's all worth it when we find the fossils that we're looking for. It's incredible to think that as we carefully and slowly remove the fossil bones from the surrounding rock, we are the first people to ever see the remains of these dinosaurs that have been hidden in the earth for millions of years. And the sunlight that shines down on them is the first light that has touched these fossils since the dinosaurs were alive, over 65 million years ago!

Stephen and Sylvia Czerkas with one of their creations, a fierce Allosaurus. *Photo credit: Mary Weikert/Star-News.*

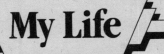

My Life
With The Dinosaurs

by Stephen and Sylvia Czerkas

A Byron Preiss Book

PUBLISHED BY POCKET BOOKS

New York   London   Toronto   Sydney   Tokyo

Special thanks to Pat MacDonald, Howard Zimmerman,
and Gwendolyn Smith.

Book design by Alex Jay/Studio J
Mechanicals by Mary LeCleir
Typesetting by David E. Seham Associates Inc.

Editor: Ruth Ashby

A MINSTREL PAPERBACK *ORIGINAL*

A Minstrel Book published by
POCKET BOOKS, a division of Simon & Schuster Inc.
1230 Avenue of the Americas, New York, NY 10020

ISBN: 0-671-63454-2

First Minstrel Books Printing March 1989

10 9 8 7 6 5 4 3 2 1

INTRODUCTION

We were getting closer to our goal each day. My wife, Sylvia, and I were on a scientific trip that had taken us over 6,000 miles from our home in Los Angeles, California. We were in the wide-open territory of Patagonia, a remote and beautiful part of southern Argentina. It was thrilling to be visiting this wonderful country, so far from our own. And it was all the more exciting to realize that after years of hoping, we were finally living one of our dreams.

We were on a dinosaur hunt, a search for the fossilized remains of giant prehistoric reptiles. I was looking not just for bones, but for one of the rarest of fossils, the skin impressions of dinosaurs. Fossils are the remains of animals or plants that lived millions of years ago. Their shape is preserved in the stone of the earth's crust. When an animal dies, the soft parts of its body decay. Usually the bone is broken up and scattered by the wind and the rain. But if the skeleton is covered by mud, the bones are not completely broken up. Water filled with minerals slowly seeps into all the cracks and holes in the bone. Eventually, these minerals completely replace the bone with stone. This stone is called fossilized bone. When we talk about dinosaur bones, we are really talking about fossils.

A fossil of dinosaur skin from a plant-eating dinosaur. Collection: National Museum of Natural Sciences, Ottawa, Canada.

Bones aren't the only things that turn into fossils. Footprints in the stone are fossils and so are skin impressions. They are rare because the soft skin is usually one of the first parts of the animal to decay. But sometimes the skin will be preserved long enough for minerals to replace it with stone. This fossil skin shows what dinosaurs really looked like. That's why, in February 1988, Sylvia and I were on the track of these hard-to-find fossils.

Our quest had begun two years earlier, when Sylvia and I attended a lecture at the local museum of natural history. It was a special event. Dr. José Bonaparte, an Argentine scientist, was describing some of the incredible fossils and dinosaurs that he had found in his homeland. Sylvia and I had already been studying dinosaurs for many years, and were quite familiar with the subject. But the dinosaurs that Dr. Bonaparte was talking about were new to science, and especially fascinating.

He described one newly discovered dinosaur that he had named *Carnotaurus*, which means "meat-eating bull." This was a good name for the dinosaur, because it not only ate meat, but it was also crowned with two large horns. These decorated the top of the skull, just over the openings where the eyes would have been. In life, this dinosaur must have looked quite frightening. While describing this dinosaur, Dr. Bonaparte mentioned that he had also found fossil skin impressions on parts of the rock that surrounded the bones. This was an incredible discovery. Fossil skin had been found for many other types of dinosaurs, but they were all plant-eaters. The fossil skin impressions of the *Carnotaurus* were our first complete impressions of a meat-eating dinosaur.

My specialty is studying fossil skin to find out what

dinosaurs really looked like. Even as a child I remember wanting to know exactly how dinosaurs looked, because I wasn't satisfied with the cartoon images of dinosaurs that were so common at the time. Of course they were fun, but I wondered if it was possible to know what dinosaurs *really* looked like, or if all the images of dinosaurs were only from someone's imagination. As a child I wondered, "Has anyone ever seen a real dinosaur?" Now I not only know that the answer to this question is "yes," but I have also become one of the people who search for real dinosaurs.

Before meeting Dr. Bonaparte, I had studied the fossilized skin impressions of dinosaurs for many years. After we got to know each other, Dr. Bonaparte asked if I would return with him to the site where he had found the *Carnotaurus*. He said that there we might find some fossil skin impressions that had been overlooked when the *Carnotaurus* was dug out of the ground. It seemed a slim chance, but I jumped at it.

A few months later, Sylvia and I were with Dr. Bonaparte in a truck, driving for days into the interior of Patagonia. Traveling with us was one of Dr. Bonaparte's assistants, Rudolfo Coria. Rudolfo was not only well educated, but he was also blessed with a clever, dry sense of humor. In a short period of time we all became close friends as well as co-workers. We became more excited the closer we came to the *Carnotaurus* site. Every evening we would stop at an *estancia,* or ranch, where we would be welcomed and invited to spend the night. The ranchers were always friendly and helpful.

When we had reached the *estancia* that was nearest the site, we set up a base camp where we could stay for several days. From our camp, it was still a few miles drive until we reached an area where we had to get out and walk. It was an awesome and desolate place, and yet there was a remarkable beauty in the surrounding rock formations. We left the truck and headed on foot into a valley. A couple of hours passed. Finally, Dr. Bonaparte pointed to a distant cliff and said, "There it is, that's where we found the *Carnotaurus.*"

Stephen working on fossils of Carnotaurus *skin at the site in Patagonia.*

It was still a couple of hundred yards away, but we were finally there. Soon we would know if our long journey would bring the reward we were after. The others set down their packs and gear at the base of a cliff and took a brief rest. I climbed up the rocks and reached the pit from which the fossils had been dug. I scanned the broken rocks within it. To my amazement, almost immediately I saw a large stone block that had the shape and outline of a scapula, which is the large bone of the shoulder. The fossil had already been removed from the block. But on it was what I had hoped to find. Located all around where the scapula had been were the impressions of the *Carnotaurus's* skin. I hollered down to everyone, "We did it! I've found more skin!"

Sylvia, Rudolfo, and Dr. Bonaparte all hurried to see what I had found. This was only the beginning. We continued to find more and more rocks that not only had the outlines of where the fossils were pried out, but also had the delicate patterns and impressions of the fossil skin. For the next three days we uncovered and examined all of the stones that had come from the pit. When we were done, we had discovered much more skin than had originally been collected. Our discovery was the first of its kind. Science finally had a good example of how the skin of a meat-eating dinosaur looked.

After leaving the *Carnotaurus* site, we continued on to other places where assistants of Dr. Bonaparte had been searching for fossils. Over the next two weeks we saw many interesting digs and dinosaur fossils. We also made many new friends. All in all, our trip to Argentina was both a successful search and an exciting and personally rewarding experience.

Later I used these skin impressions and Dr. Bonaparte's other fossil finds to make a sculpture of the *Carnotaurus*. This is what it looks like:

The mystery is solved: Stephen's sculpture of a Carnotaurus *was reconstructed with fossil clues from the past. Without a realistic skin texture, this ferocious dinosaur would not look so alive!*

Traveling to different parts of the world, visiting museums, or going out on dinosaur digs are just part of what Sylvia and I do in our work. When we are back home we continue our research, "digging" through reference books. There is a great deal of studying. But even this is thrilling. Like detectives, we solve mysteries and gain our information from ancient fossilized clues to the past.

Sylvia and I are quite fortunate in being able to work for museums, researching and digging up dinosaur fossils and creating models of the great beasts. We have a career that is often fun and exciting. Working in any science is interesting, but, like many other people, we have a special fascination with dinosaurs.

CHAPTER 1

"Where are the dinosaurs?"

That is the first question asked by most young people as they enter a natural history museum. Dinosaurs have been a source of wonder since they were first identified. That was back in the 1840s. Some dinosaur bones had been discovered before then, but nobody knew what kind of animals they were from.

It is not just their size that amazes people. It is that dinosaurs lived so many years ago. Imagine animals that lived before your great-great-great- grandparents and many generations before that. Imagine animals that lived before mammals ruled the earth. Then try to imagine animals that lived millions and millions of years ago. That's when dinosaurs were alive.

Thinking about dinosaurs is like visiting another world of another time. Sylvia and I explore that world every day. We are paleontologists, people who study ancient life. The word "paleontology" comes from the

Greek language, and means the study of ancient life. I am a paleo*artist*. I make sculptures of dinosaurs for museum exhibits, and have made dinosaurs for the movies. Sylvia is a paleoartist as well, and we enjoy working together. She is also a curator, which is someone who helps conserve, or take care of things. Her specialty is art dealing with the dinosaurs.

In our work, we try to make dinosaurs seem alive again. We take all the information that has ever been learned about dinosaurs and put it into our sculptures. We want to create dinosaurs so real-looking that people can imagine what they were like.

It's true that a picture is worth a thousand words. A person looking at a painting or sculpture of a dinosaur can learn about it on many levels at once. What does the dinosaur look like? What is he doing? What kind of environment is he in? These questions can all be answered by one visual image.

You may be thinking that everyone *knows* what dinosaurs look like. You've seen them in comic books, in movies, in magazines. Why make more pictures of dinosaurs?

In some cases, what you've seen is wrong, and our information about dinosaurs is growing all the time. And when we learn something new, we try to correct past mistakes. Take, for example, the huge *Tyrannosaurus rex* at the American Museum of Natural History in New York City. The fossilized bones of this dinosaur, one of the most frightening that ever lived,

Sylvia's version of the Tyrannosaurus rex.

were dug up in Hell Creek, Montana, in 1908 and taken to New York. They were put together in the museum to show the dinosaur in an upright position, standing as tall as possible. It looks as if it's trying to walk like John Wayne. The problem is—its posture is not correct! The *Tyrannosaurus* might have been able to stand that high sometimes, if it wanted to reach for something. But its normal walking position would have been much more horizontal. And its tail would have been held up above the ground, instead of dragging behind it.

Scientists even eighty years ago suspected that the skeleton of the *Tyrannosaurus* was not totally correct. Scientists today are changing the image of the dinosaurs that we all grew up with. Paleoartists like Sylvia and me are working with the scientists to make that image more correct. Together, we put "flesh" on the bare bones of the dinosaurs and bring them to life.

By working together, scientists and artists have shown people what dinosaurs looked like. This has been going on for the past 150 years.

Before that, the fossils of dinosaurs were not understood. Their discovery gave rise to wonderful stories of mythical monsters. When petrified dinosaur bones, or fossils, were first found, people thought they were dragons' teeth, or the bones of giants. Scientific study of these fossils did not begin until the start of the nineteenth century. Even then, no one realized how old these huge bones were, or what kind of animals they belonged to.

The turning point, or so the story goes, came one fine spring day in 1822. Mary Ann Mantell, the wife of a young doctor, was walking along an English country road. She saw something that looked like a tooth sticking out of a rock. Excited, she showed it to her husband, who was a fossil hunter. Gideon Mantell was sure they had made an important discovery.

He declared they had found the tooth of a giant extinct reptile. He named the reptile *Iguanodon,* which means "iguana tooth," because the tooth looked like that of the modern iguana.

At first the scientists would not believe Mantell. But in 1841, after several other discoveries, the ancient beasts were given a new name. British scientist

Sir Richard Owen called the giant reptiles, Dinosauria, which means "terrible reptiles." (This doesn't mean they were bad, it means they were ferocious.)

Today we know that dinosaurs lived during the three periods of the Mesozoic era: the Triassic, the Jurassic, and the Cretaceous. They first appeared on Earth about 220 million years ago and died out 65 million years ago. What caused the dinosaurs to die out is still a mystery. There are several new ideas, but they haven't yet been proven.

It didn't take long after *Iguanodon* was discovered until many other dinosaurs surfaced. *Megalosaurus* and *Hylaeosaurus* were recognized as dinosaurs about the same time as *Iguanodon*. Fossils of the tiny *Compsognathus* and the reptile-bird *Archeopteryx* were found later in 1861. Then came some magnificent discoveries in the American West.

Two rival paleontologists, Othniel Charles Marsh of Yale University and Edward Drinker Cope of Philadelphia, fought a fierce "bone war" to see who could collect the most fossils. Fossil hunters on both sides dug for dinosaurs the year round, enduring rainstorms, blizzards, and rockslides. The results were tremendous. Tons and tons of fossils were shipped east from the massive dinosaur graveyards in the western states. Among them were the first fossils of many of the better-known dinosaurs, including the *Apatosaurus* (*Apatosaurus* is the correct scientific name for the long-necked dinosaurs commonly known

TIMELINE

Million years B.C.

	1.8 Quaternary	Age of man	present–1.8 million years
	65 Tertiary	Hoofed animals and apes appear	1.8–65
MESOZOIC ERA: AGE OF THE DINOSAURS	144 Cretaceous	First flowering plants Last dinosaurs	65–144
	213 Jurassic	Middle dinosaurs	144–213
	248 Triassic	First dinosaurs First mammals	213–248
	286 Permian		248–286
	360 Carboniferous		286–360
	408 Devonian	First amphibians	360–408
	438 Silurian	First land plants	408–438
	505 Ordovician		438–505
	590 Cambrian		505–590
	4.6 billion Pre-Cambrian	Early life on Earth	590–4.6 billion years

Remember: for prehistoric times, the higher the number, the farther back in time! For example, 200 million B.C. is longer ago than 65 million B.C.

A scale model of Waterhouse Hawkins' Iguanodon.

as *Brontosaurs*. The first *Apatosaurus* skeleton found was very incomplete, so when another similar but more complete skeleton was discovered it was thought to be a different animal and was given the name of *Brontosaurus*. Later, scientists realized that *Brontosaurus* was the same animal as *Apatosaurus,* and that the first name of *Apatosaurus* was the correct name for both of them.), the *Triceratops,* the *Allosaurus,* the *Stegosaurus,* and the *Diplodocus.* The dinosaur had once again come into its own, after millions of years.

The bones fascinated the public. But people wanted

Mural by Charles R. Knight showing a battle between a Tyrannosaurus rex *and a* Triceratops. *Photo courtesy of the Field Museum of Natural History, and the artist, Charles R. Knight, (Neg# CK59442) Chicago.*

to know: what did the dinosaurs really look like when they were alive? Experts didn't wait long to reconstruct them. Sir Richard Owen formed the first successful scientist/artist partnership with Waterhouse Hawkins, a fine sculptor and painter. Hawkins made the first life-size sculpture of the *Iguanodon.* Actually it was much larger than life, because not enough *Iguanodon* fossils had been discovered to be able to tell the dinosaur's true size. The reconstruction made the *Iguanodon* look something like a giant rhinoceros.

Owen and Hawkins threw a party to celebrate the creation of the sculpture. They sent out invitations designed in the shape of a *Pterodactyl* wing. And they had a multi-course dinner—inside the partially finished sculpture! Owen himself sat at the head of the *Iguanodon.*

The *Iguanodon* was a magnificent sculpture, and so were the others Owen and Hawkins went on to create.

16

They put into these pieces a great deal of imagination and all of their scientific knowledge. They made some mistakes because they had so little fossil evidence to go on. But they also were amazingly correct about many things!

The second important scientist/artist team was Henry Fairfield Osborn and Charles R. Knight. Osborn was the president of the American Museum of Natural History in New York City during the early twentieth century. He worked closely with Knight to create paintings and murals for the museum.

In the half century that had gone by since Owens' and Hawkins' work, thousands of dinosaur bones had been dug up, especially in the American West. Osborn and Knight had a great deal to work with. More than anyone else, Knight gave us our popular image of the dinosaur. Through newspapers, magazines, books, and postcards, his pictures of dinosaurs went out all over the world.

People grew used to the images of the four most popular dinosaurs—ferocious *Tyrannosaurus rex,* long-necked *Apatosaurus,* armor-plated *Stegosaurus,* and horned *Triceratops.* But, perhaps because of World War Two, popular interest in the dinosaurs dropped off during the late 1940s and early 1950s.

In the 1950s, Rudolph Zalinger painted a huge, 110 foot-long mural for the Peabody Museum of Natural History at Yale. The mural was reprinted in a foldout in *LIFE* magazine, and it inspired many children to become paleontologists! In the 1960s and 1970s, there was a renewed interest in dinosaurs and their world. And today there are more people working on dinosaurs than ever before.

New information discovered about dinosaurs in the last twenty years has caused many museum exhibits to be redone. All over the world, new dinosaur halls and exhibits are being built. It's a great time to be a paleoartist or paleontologist.

Our dinosaur studies have taken me and Sylvia all over the world. We have hunted for dinosaurs in North America and South America. We have worked with artists in Taiwan, recreating life-size dinosaurs. We have also traveled with our dinosaur art and sculptures throughout the United States, Canada, and the United Kingdom. Our many research trips to find out what dinosaurs looked like have taken us to museums throughout the world.

Sylvia and I discovered our interest in dinosaurs in different ways. Here's how it happened.

CHAPTER 2

I've known that I wanted to be a paleontologist since I was four years old. That's when I saw my first picture of a dinosaur—and instantly wanted to know more about them.

My family and I had gone to a big family get-together at my Uncle Ozzie's and Aunt Lois's. While there I stumbled across a book on dinosaurs that belonged to my cousin Terry. Instantly, I became fascinated with the pictures and wanted to have that book.

I was told I couldn't have it. But I could enjoy it for the rest of the day. My Uncle Keith pointed out names of the dinosaurs in bold-face type, and read them to me. I was so young that reading was a whole new idea.

Since I didn't know if I'd ever see a book on dinosaurs again, I decided to keep a record. When I saw a typewriter in the house I simply matched the letters of the names in the book to the keys, and made

Stephen as a young boy.

a list of all the dinosaurs in the book. The family was very impressed, and I heard this story several times while I was growing up. After a while this became only a distant childhood memory, and I couldn't tell whether I remembered it the way it had actually happened or the way it had been told to me. Then, about five or six years ago, my mother gave me a family photo album as a Christmas gift. As I turned the pages I found the list of dinosaur names! She had kept it for me all those years. All of my memories were true.

I was born in Alhambra, California, in 1951. I was the youngest of three children, with an older sister, Crystal, and an older brother, Joseph. We were all very close and had loving parents.

My father, Victor Czerkas, was a commercial artist

```
diplovertebron
                              123456789
dimetrodon

   io hthyosaurus
   stegosaurs
      albosaurus
  ddiplodocus
  brachiosaurus
              archaeopteryx
         pteranodon
       hesperornis
       tylosaurus
       trachodon
      protoceratops
           triceratops
         parasaur Olophus
         tyrannosaurus
             palaeoscincus
            archelon
            eOhippus
        me sonyx
           notharctus
           brontops
ba luohitherium m
    aitic amelus
    smilo don
            megather ium
       wooly  rhinoceros
       mastodon
```

Stephen's childhood list of dinosaurs.

for the movie industry, and a fine artist in his own right. As a young man he had come from Sioux City, Iowa, to work in Hollywood's movie industry. He started out doing set design. Rather than go to real places, movie crews often build sets of them on a stage. My father was an artist who painted the background scenery of clouds, mountains, trees, cities, or whatever was needed. Years later, he became a title artist, designing and making the artwork and lettering for movies and television shows. He was responsible

Stephen with his father, Victor Czerkas.

for the titles of some of the earliest TV shows, which were filmed live in those days. I remember visiting him at the studio, where I would often see some of the behind-the-scenes of movie making. I remember watching with special interest the titles of many television shows like "Have Gun Will Travel," "Gunsmoke," "Mission: Impossible," "Mannix," "Hawaii 5-O," and the original "Star Trek." My dad had designed them. Before this, dad worked at Universal Pictures and made the titles for films like *The Creature of the Black Lagoon*.

My mother, Shirley Czerkas, was a working housewife who took care of the kids while we were growing up. No small task. My brother and I had the usual arguments. But generally we were a close and happy family. My mother and father saw to that.

When I was barely a teenager, my sister married Det Merryman. I really looked up to him as another big brother. A few years after they had a baby girl, Ashley. Today, Ashley is a beautiful young woman who is studying film at the University of Southern California and is actively working on motion pictures. Det and Cris have always been involved with the arts and entertainment, and with publishing as well.

When I was growing up, my family life was happy enough to make TV's "Leave It to Beaver" family envious. But tragedy has also struck my family. My brother Joseph developed cancer and died at the age of only twenty-four. Joseph also left behind his loving wife, Wanda. For all of us, the death of my brother was the most shattering thing that we have ever endured. Joe was more than just a good man, he was a person of strength and character, with a gentle heart. Joe was studying to become a lawyer. Not a day goes by that he isn't missed, we all loved him so much.

Memories are the valued gifts of a lifetime. I remember playing in the yard with my brother and other friends as some of the happiest times in my life. I was fortunate to have such a wonderful childhood. I can remember how happy I was when I spent a day with

Older brother Joseph and Stephen during a Christmas gift opening.

my dad painting pictures in the park. My parents have always encouraged my artistic talents.

This was great, because as soon as I discovered dinosaurs I decided I wanted to make my own. I went out to the backyard, added water to dirt, and made dinosaurs out of the mud. Since mud figures collapse easily, I was limited to low-to-the-ground dinosaurs, such as *Anklyosaurs*.

Soon after, my parents bought me some clay. With air-dried clay I made dinosaurs that I could actually play with—at least until the arms and legs broke off.

I always wanted Santa Claus to bring dinosaurs that were posable—that is, dinosaurs that could move in different directions. Nowadays, children can find such dinosaur toys in any toy store. But when I was young, you were very lucky if you could find any dinosaur models at all. When I did have models, I would always cut them apart, put them in better poses, and then melt the pieces back together at the family stove. Many evenings the smell of burning wax and plastic would float through the entire house. Considering the messes that I sometimes made, the family was very understanding.

I was trying to make the models moveable so I could play with them better. Oddly enough, that later became my profession. For about twelve years, I made moveable monsters and posed dinosaurs frame-by-frame for the movies.

I was always pleased to receive a bag of plastic

dinosaurs as a Christmas or birthday present. My brother wasn't interested in dinosaurs, so he would get a bag of soldiers. We'd have great battles on the floor, with hundreds of dinosaurs against hundreds of soldiers!

Sadly for me, modern weapons would always win, and the dinosaurs would lose the battles. But we'd always fight about the outcome—I never could believe a single rifle bullet could kill a dinosaur.

When I was about seven years old, we drove out to Iowa to visit some relatives. On the way we passed a sign with a great green *Brontosaurus* on it. It read: "Dinosaur National Monument, 800 miles."

"Hey Mom, look at that," I shouted.

Then, hours later, came, "Dinosaur National Monument, 600 miles." "Mom, Mom, it's getting closer!"

Then, "Dinosaur National Monument, 500 miles. Turn right." "Hey Mom, turn!"

We didn't turn. For the next two weeks of the trip, there was a little child crying in the backseat. I felt as if the chance of a lifetime had passed me by.

Well, the next summer my parents kindly—and wisely—decided to take the whole family that extra 500 miles. The Dinosaur National Monument is right outside the city of Vernal, Utah. Vernal has dinosaur things everywhere. There are many lifesize dinosaur sculptures outside the motels and throughout the town. For the family, it was a fun place to visit. But for me, it was truly exciting.

The monument mentioned in the road signs is a museum where they have exhibits about the dinosaurs. Here you can see the bones actually sticking out of the cliff where they are still being dug out of the rock. As far as I knew then, this was where *all* dinosaurs came from. Seeing the bones in the cliff made me realize dinosaurs were real animals who had actually existed. This was a major turning point in my life.

The credit for the next turning point should go to my brother. He was sitting in the den one day, watching TV, when I came in. "Hey, you should watch this!" he said. It was *King Kong!* I came in on the part where King Kong is on stage, trying to break out of his chains and about to crash through New York City. I was amazed at what I saw. This was the first monster movie I'd ever watched.

I waited patiently for over a year until the giant gorilla was on TV again. I found out that the movie was called *King Kong.* Much to my surprise, there were dinosaurs in the beginning of the movie, the part that I had missed before. Naturally, *King Kong* became my favorite movie of all time. I must have seen it a hundred times over the years.

I asked my dad how they made *King Kong.* He explained that the monsters were all movable minatures. To make a minature seem to come alive, the movie crew would move it a bit and shoot one frame of film. Then they would move it again, and shoot again. And again, and again. This process is called stop-motion photography. This was all the information I could get. Nowadays, you can find magazines and books that tell all about special movie effects. But back then, special effects were not popular and there was little information on the subject.

As a child I had many friends, but I was the only one interested in dinosaurs, or in movie-making and special effects. I remember a few annoying kids calling me the "monster man." It's satisfying to see that what I was doing then is very popular today.

With the money that I saved from my paper route,

From left to right: Stephen, his mother, Shirley Czerkas, sister, Crystal, and brother, Joseph.

I was able to buy a used movie camera from the local drugstore. It was not only difficult to find a movie camera that I could afford, but I also had to be selective and make sure that the movie camera could take one picture at a time. This was very important if I was to make films with moveable miniatures. After weeks of looking, I finally found my first camera. It was a simple eight millimeter with a single lens, but it could do what I wanted, and photograph one frame at a time.

Weekends and summer months were times when I spent many hours experimenting and working with my camera. I couldn't find information on how to make animated movies, so I had to learn by trial and error. I would make models out of wire and wooden joints, and then move them just a bit for each frame of film. By moving the model just a fraction of an inch, photographing it, and then repeating the process, I was able to bring my models to life in short movies.

When I was twelve years old, I entered one of my movies in a national contest sponsored by Kodak. It was a complete movie, about fifteen minutes long. Oddly enough, it didn't have any dinosaurs in it, but it did have a dragon, a skeleton sword fight, and a mythical Greek flying creature. These were all out of movies I had seen, mostly those made by special-effects wizard Ray Harryhausen. I made complete skeletons, about six inches high, with every bone in place. The dragon was about five and a half feet long, with a three-foot-long tail. It took me an entire summer just to do the tail, because each scale was stamped individually into the clay, and there were hundreds of scales.

Times haven't changed that much. I still sculpt each scale individually on my models.

The idea for my movie script came from monster magazines, of which I was an avid collector. I had to sneak them into the house, because my mother didn't approve of them.

In my script, a little boy reads the monster magazines and falls asleep. He dreams about the monsters—and they become a little too real! In his dream, the monsters come alive and he fights with them. Of course, I called the movie *Nightmare*. I asked the local actor down the block, a little boy who was younger than I was, to be the dreamer. He thought it would be great fun, and my dad actually created and drew the titles for the film.

I was twelve years old when I made that film. And it won an award, even though the contest in which I entered it was supposed to be for teenagers only. This encouraged me to continue making movies.

My parents were always very supportive of my interst in dinosaurs and movies. But my school teachers were not.

In grammer school, I would always draw dinosaurs in art class. Back in the 1950s, boys were guided to draw things like sports or trucks, and the girls to draw flowers or houses. But I drew dinosaurs. I drew so many dinosaurs that teachers would actually complain about it, saying, "Can't you do anything else?" Of course I could. But what I *liked* was doing dinosaurs!

One summer, my parents sent me to an art class in Pasadena. They thought the class would help to develop my talent. But the teacher was very concerned about my art. He pulled my mother aside one morning and said, "I want to discuss a problem with your son. He only wants to draw dinosaurs! As a parent you may not know this, but have you ever heard of paleontology?"

"Of course," my mother answered. "That's what Stephen wants to do when he grows up."

The teacher wasn't satisfied with that at all. He wanted me to draw other things besides dinosaurs. But my mother stood up for me, as she always has.

I had similar run-ins all the way through school, in which the teachers just didn't understand. Though they had good intentions, they got in the way of what I wanted to learn.

When I was fifteen, I made a clay sculpture of a *Stegosaurus* that was almost three feet long. It was as accurate as I could make it, with glass eyes and every scale in place. My mother liked it so much that she called the Los Angeles County Museum and arranged to have the professional paleontologists see it. The visit should have encouraged me to become a paleontologist too.

We went, and the curators praised my model. They took us on an exciting tour of the back rooms of the museum, where the bones were kept. But when I told the paleontologists that I wanted to grow up and be like them, they told me it was very difficult for anyone to make a living as a paleontologist.

To this day, I'm not sure why they were so negative. But at the time I was very upset. For at least ten years, I didn't think of becoming a paleontologist. There were no courses available in paleontology in the two years I spent at Pasadena City College, so I had no idea how to pursue my scientific interests in dinosaurs.

But I still had to make a living, and I knew I could do that working on movies.

CHAPTER 3

Ray Harryhausen was one of the heroes of my childhood. He was the special effects genius who made movie monsters come alive. His movies—*The Seventh Voyage of Sinbad, First Men in the Moon, Mysterious Island, Jason and the Argonauts*—were the direct inspiration for many of the models I made in my youth. The day I met Ray was the next turning point in my life.

When I was just out of high school, I tracked down the editor of my favorite childhood magazine, *Famous Monsters of Filmland*. His name was Forrest J. Ackerman and I knew that he had a great collection of monster-movie stuff, and that he would be an interesting person to meet. One day I found his address and drove to his house. I had no idea what to expect.

I rang the bell on his front door. In one hand I held a *Pterodactyl* with a two-foot-long wingspan; in the other, a bag full of my stop-motion dinosaur models. The door opened, and Ackerman himself came out.

He looked down at me and saw the *Pterodactyl* in my hand.

"Hello?" I said uncertainly.

"Come in, come in," Ackerman answered automatically. "Show me what you've got!"

He was one of the kindest and most encouraging men I'd ever met. He spent the whole afternoon with me and showed me his science-fiction and monster-movie collection. I saw the *King Kong* models and *Lost World* models that animator Willis O'Brien used to make these movie classics. As I was leaving, Forry turned to me and said, "Would you like to meet Ray Harryhausen next week?"

You bet I would!

The following week I returned to Forry's house. There I found forty to fifty other people waiting outside the front door. Ray Harryhausen was living in Europe then, so his visits to Los Angeles were rare. I had no idea who these people were, but they had to be Harryhausen fans, just like I was. Finally, Ray and Forry drove up in a car, and the crowd got very excited, just as if he were a rock star.

We all went into the house, and Ray was very friendly and encouraging. He didn't say much about how he performed his movie magic, but it was wonderful for all of us to talk with him and show him the models that we had brought.

This was the first time I had met other people who were also doing special effects and animation. We went around saying to each other, "Gee, you do that, too?" We were mostly teenagers and young men in our early twenties. That day I met Jim Danforth, David Allen, Phil Tippet, and Dennis Muren. Today they are all famous animators and special-effects creators for the movies.

That was also the day I met Jim Aupperle. We became friends and partners who worked together for a good twelve years. I would sculpt models and he would do the lighting and photography, and we would both take turns "animating" the models. That is, moving them a bit for each frame of film.

For a while, Jim and I worked on a lot of small, low-budget movies. I would go from movie studio to studio, looking for jobs. I used an easy technique. While waiting at a studio entrance, I would hold a three-foot spider or an armful of dinosaur models. Glamorous actors and actresses would also wait outside the studio entrance, hoping for the chance to be noticed and asked inside. Eventually, some bigshot from the studio would notice my models and say, "Hey, that's really neat. Are you doing that for so-and-so?" naming someone I didn't know. "No," I'd answer, "do you think he'd be interested?"

The next thing you knew, the spider and I would be on the other side of the studio gate, while a gorgeous actor or actress would still be outside waiting. I didn't get all that many jobs, but I did meet a lot of people!

The special effects team for Planet of Dinosaurs. *From left to right: Jim Aupperle, Stephen, and Doug Beswick.*

Eventually Jim and I found someone who wanted to direct and produce his own movies. His name was James K. Shea, and he had never made a movie before. He was very enthusiastic about the special effects that we could do, and he decided to work with us on making a feature film. Shea had more determination than just about any other person I have ever met, and he made his plans work.

Overcoming incredible odds, we all worked together long days and nights to make our dream a reality. Since we had no track record, it took us two years to raise the money for the movie, and another two years to make it. We raised just enough money to make one of the smallest-budget movies ever, *Planet of Dinosaurs*. The acting wasn't very good and the script wasn't much better, but the special effects were very good and quite plentiful. We paced the film so that as soon as the audience might be ready to get up and leave, there was another dinosaur scene. That would keep people entertained, we thought.

And they were. The movie was bought for showing all over the world, and today it is still available, on videotape. Universal Studios even used it in their tour as an example of stop-motion photography.

Stephen discussing an animation project with Jim Shea and Ray Harryhausen.

Battle scene between a Stegosaurus *and* Allosaurus *from Stephen's feature film* Planet of Dinosaurs.

Jim and I spent four years perfecting the kind of stop-motion used by Ray Harryhausen and Willis O'Brien (the animator who created King Kong). We refined everything to really professional quality, under severe restrictions, the hardest of which was a lack of money. But just like similar special-effects movies that are fortunate enough to have a sizeable budget, we did the stop-motion frame by frame. If we got five seconds of footage by the end of a day, we were happy. It was often a painful and draining experience. But we eventually completed the film. The years of hard work paid off. Even though we didn't make millions of dollars like Steven Spielberg, we didn't lose money, and we did learn a great deal in the process.

After that movie, Jim and I looked for something else to do. We went over to Filmation Studios with some sample footage from our movie. They were impressed. Filmation was doing a weekly TV series for kids using stop-motion techniques. The show was called "Jason of Star Command," and we worked there for two years. That was the best professional time Jim and I had. It was a happy crew, and we had a lot of control over what we did and how we did it.

And what about dinosaurs during this time? Well, I did a lot of small models for movies. I even kept up

Stephen at Filmation Studios, working on a dog creature for Jason of Star Command.

A test shot for Stephen's Apotasaurus *animation model.*

on my dinosaur comic book collection. I remember
once going into a comic bookstore and asking about
their *Turok, Son of Stone* comics. They had a few,
but their other dinosaur stuff had all been grabbed up
by someone named George Olshevsky. The sales-
person thought we'd have a lot in common, and suggested that George and I meet each other.

So I left my phone number, and a week later George
called. We started talking about dinosaurs and he told
me about a group that met in L.A. called The Dinosaur
Society. He suggested I call up the hostess and invite
myself over.

Well, that wasn't the sort of thing I usually did. But

I really wanted to see what The Dinosaur Society was all about. So I made the call and went over to the house that weekend. I got there kind of early—and Sylvia answered the door. Of course, we fell in love immediately, and then . . .

But Sylvia has her own version of this story, and what led her to that moment.

CHAPTER 4

When I was a child, I had one advantage that Stephen didn't have. In my backyard we had Michigan clay instead of California dirt. My mother and I would dig up the clay and sculpt animals—especially birds, with their nests and eggs. Then we would bake them out in the sun.

But I didn't make dinosaurs. Not until years later.

I was born Sylvia Piechal, in Detroit, Michigan, in 1943. My father, William Piechal, came from Poland when he was two. My mother Bernice was born in the United States but her parents were Polish. Michigan has a large community of Polish people who came over to work in the auto industry. My father worked for the auto industry as a tool and dye maker. He made perfect patterns for every part of an automobile, from every tiny nut and bolt to large engine parts. His job demanded a high degree of craftsmanship, and required him to make accurate measurements to within one-thousandth of an inch.

The Piechals, from left to right: Elaine, Sylvia, William, Bill, and Bernice.

I had a happy life as a child, with my sister, brother, mother, and dad. My mother cared for the family and worked hard keeping our home spotlessly clean. For me, she was the perfect storybook mother. She was sensitive and gentle, and the two of us were very close. We read together and talked about what we had read. Every day, like clockwork, she would do her studies—she read books on philosophy and religion, as well as history. So we had shelves of books on Buddhism and Christianity and Greek philosophy. It was wonderful having someone so thoughtful and sensitive in my life. It was a shock to discover, as I did when I grew up, that everyone wasn't like my mother. She was truly a unique and special person.

My sister, Elaine, is seven years older than I, and my brother, Bill, is seven years younger. Today my sister and her husband keep an inn and antique shop in a historical building that was a wayside stagecoach stop built in 1832. My brother is the director of a hospital and a very successful doctor. Fittingly, he is an osteopath, or bone doctor!

I was a talkative child and enjoyed having lots of friends. But I also wanted to spend time by myself, because I always had so much I wanted to do. I loved reading and came home from the library each week with piles of books. I would read several each day. By the time I was ten, I think I had actually read all of Shakespeare's plays.

I was very lucky to grow up in a family that loved music and the arts. Beautiful objects were important to us. My father had a collection of wonderful Oriental carvings called *netsukes*, which he brought back from Japan after World War Two. *Netsukes* are little ivory or wood sculptures that people would hang from the sashes of their *kimonos*, or long robes. They are usually carvings of people or animals, and often very humorous. My parents kept their *netsukes* in a glass case and would let me take them out and play with them, even when I was very small. I remember one that was a favorite of mine. It was what is called a trick *netsuke*. It just looked like a house, but if you tipped it, little men would pop out of the windows.

My father brought back other beautiful pieces as

Older sister Elaine reading to Bill and Sylvia.

well—a Pekinese dog carved out of cherrywood, and an artist's brushholder carved from the tusk of an elephant. I used to spend hours just looking at all these objects.

Artistic talents were always strong in my family. Both my parents were extremely talented at doing things with their hands. My mother was an excellent seamstress, and taught me to make my own doll clothes. My father also did needlepoint and goldleafing. Gold leaf is a very thin sheet of gold that you can apply to objects by using glue and an especially soft brush. My father used to apply it to anything around the house he felt needed some improving—books, candle holders, whatever. Later when I became an artist, I used gold leaf on some of my jewelry designs as well.

The day I was introduced to classical music is one of my earliest childhood memories. A neighbor was babysitting me at her house when it came time for my nap. When I lay down on the couch, she played some classical music on the record player. It was splendid. Years later, when I was in high school, I would bicycle many miles each way to the Detroit Arts Institute to hear concerts and opera. I remember standing through an entire performance of Verdi's *Aida* after one of these marathon trips. *Aida* is four hours long! Luckily, I always had *lots* of energy.

I was involved with dance, too. My sister went to high school with a fellow down the street who was a ballet dancer. She took me to one of his performances at the Detroit Arts Institute. I thought the dancing was the most wonderful thing I had ever seen, and I really wanted to learn how to dance. So my sister's friend gave me dance lessons until he left Detroit. Then I studied dance throughout high school, and also took it in college, then at the Joseph Rickard Studio. For a while I considered becoming a professional dancer, but art eventually won out.

My first great love, when I was a child, was nature. Our house was right next to a large field. In the summer it was all wild with flowers and grasses and old tree stumps and things like that. I used to pick wild raspberries and flowers to bring home to my mother. I collected flowers and insects. I spent a lot of time just looking at the tiny details of nature, even studying the tree bark. And in the winter there was a little

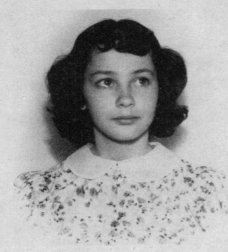

*Sylvia at
ten years old.*

pond that would freeze over, where we could go skating.

And then there were animals. I absolutely adored animals, especially dogs. My mother loved animals as much as I did, but found it too painful to part with them. Since she grew up on a farm, she knew that animals always die before people do. (An exception is the African gray parrot that Stephen and I have now. It will live to be 100 years old.) So she wouldn't let the family keep any pets.

But I found ways to sneak them into the house. When I was in elementary school, a magician came to town and performed a magic show for the children. He made hamsters disappear. He asked for volunteers, so I went up on stage to make sure that the hamsters really did vanish into thin air. As a reward, he gave me one of the vanishing hamsters! I took it home in a Tide detergent box and begged my mother to let me keep it. She finally agreed. My father made a beautiful wooden cage for it, with hinges and doors, and the hamster became a much-loved member of the family.

That hamster paved the way for other small pets. One year my science teacher gave away tadpoles, so we could bring them home and watch them turn into frogs. My mother and I prepared a special little cage for my tadpole. Everyday we smashed egg yolks into tiny pieces for the tadpole to eat. Sure enough, the tadpole started to develop legs! One warm summer day, after it had started to rain, my mother suggested we take Taddy out so it could play around in the fresh rainwater. Suddenly it started to hail, and my poor tadpole was hit by one of the biggest hailstones you've ever seen! It was smashed. My mother and I cried for hours and hours over that tadpole.

Needless to say, I never got my dog.

So, I had a rich and varied childhood. I loved animals, and I was fascinated by the arts. I liked opera, ballet, and stage plays all through my youth. At one time I thought I wanted to be an actress. I appeared in plays throughout my elementary and high school years.

But it wasn't until my late teens that I decided the visual arts would be my career. As I mentioned, I started sculpting at a very early age. I think that when someone has artistic talent, they are either a 2-D or a 3-D person. That is, either they naturally see things as lines on a piece of paper (2-D), or as forms filling a space (3-D). Stephen and I are both 3-D people. Though Stephen can draw very well, he is a great sculptor. And sculpting came easily to me. I had to work so hard at drawing that it would often give me a headache.

But they didn't teach sculpture in my high school. So I decided to teach myself. I got all the books I could find on sculpture from the library and read them very carefully. I started sculpting pieces and taught myself to make molds and things like that. Then I decided to go to college and study art.

That's why I came to California. I had read about all the different colleges around the country and heard about what a wonderful educational system they had out there. And then there was the climate. The Michigan summers are really fun, but the winters are cold, gray, and dreary. I longed for year-round sunshine.

Since I would have to pay for my own education, I went first to Los Angeles City College, where the cost is relatively low. I enjoyed it tremendously. Clyde Kelly, my ceramics instructor, was exceptionally kind to me. In ceramics class, I learned how to make objects out of clay by sculpting them and then baking them in a very hot oven called a kiln. To make the surface of the pottery shiny and hard, I would apply a coating called a glaze before putting the object in

Sylvia sculpting a woolly mammoth.

the kiln. Mr. Kelly let me fire the kiln and mix glazes and help around the lab. And he let me take as much clay home as I wanted to. So, of course I made about ten times more things than anybody else. Also, I learned all about chemical glaze formulas. I never was interested in math until I found a practical application for it. I studied glaze chemistry, clay composition, and where the clays were found, and made hundreds of things out of clay! Then I went on to take all my other sculpture and design courses.

After I transferred to the state college, I had another wonderful teacher, Joe Soldate. He gave me free access to the lab, so I could go in and sculpt whatever I wanted.

I was very fortunate in my education in having people who cared about and encouraged me. I think having someone supporting you makes a big difference in anyone's career. That's where Stephen's education differs from mine.

Even before I left school, I was able to sell my sculptures to art galleries. After I graduated, I developed a successful business. I was one of the first artists to work with a man-made plastic material. I learned most of my techniques from industry, because at that time plastics were hardly ever used by artists. As opposed to working with bronze, which is smelly and dirty and even dangerous if you do the casting yourself, plastics are easier to control. They are lightweight and long-lasting.

Over the years, I developed my artistic skills and specialized in jewelry and sculptures. My jewelry used ladies' faces and animals designed as pins. I would mix plastic resin with marble dust so that the jewelry looked as if it were made out of ivory. The *netsukes* of my childhood had made me love the look of ivory.

I was always more interested in doing sculptures of people and animals than in abstract art. At first I specialized in the living animals of today. But I soon became interested in endangered species and then switched to extinct animals, such as woolly mammoths, saber-toothed cats, and dodo birds.

For years I worked mostly on extinct animals. Then, in 1975, I discovered the most extinct animal of all—the dinosaur. My first sculpture was of a baby *Protoceratops* coming out of its shell. It was based on

Beauty and Beast pin, an example of Sylvia's jewelry.

Elephant by Sylvia.

Dodo by Sylvia.

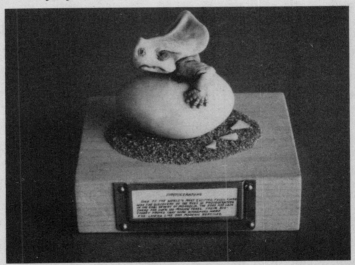

Sylvia's first dinosaur sculpture, a Protoceratops *coming out of its shell.*

one of the most exciting dinosaur fossil finds ever. Nests of *Protoceratops* eggs were found in China's Gobi Desert in the 1920s. Until those discoveries, it was not known that dinosaurs actually laid eggs.

Dinosaurs were the most interesting animals that I had ever studied, and I was fascinated. From there on, I really never looked back. I created only dinosaurs.

I also started studying the art and literature of dinosaurs for the first time. That's how I came across Charles R. Knight. As Stephen mentioned before, Knight was the greatest painter of prehistoric life during the first half of the twentieth century. I discovered that no one had ever written a book about him. So, with the encouragement of a paleontologist friend, Robert Long, Don Glut and I decided that the time had come to write a book. Don and I worked on the book together. Then, as I located and collected Charles Knight's major paintings and drawings, it seemed natural to put together an exhibit of them. Thus the Charles R. Knight show was born. So far, the exhibit has traveled to fifteen cities—and is still traveling.

Putting together an exhibit for museums involves so much work getting things framed, writing to people, and arranging for loans, that I found it a full-time job. Also, the Charles R. Knight show inspired me. It made me want to put together an exhibit of all the best dinosaur art that has ever been done. The Natural

History Museum of Los Angeles County was impressed by the Charles R. Knight exhibit. So, when they wanted to put on a new dinosaur exhibit, they asked me to be the curator and put the exhibit together for them. I explained my concept, which was to show how artists and scientists had worked together to picture dinosaurs, from their first discovery until the present day. The director of the museum, Dr. Craig Black, liked this approach very much, so it became my job to gather together the finest dinosaur illustrations.

"Dinosaurs Past and Present" became the largest exhibit of dinosaur art ever brought together. It includes a model of Waterhouse Hawkins' original *Iguanodon,* and paintings by Charles R. Knight. It also has paintings and sculptures by today's top dinosaur artists, people like Mark Hallett, Douglas Henderson, John Gurche, Gregory Paul, Eleanor Kish, Ron Seguin, Vladimir Krb, the Zallingers, Margaret Colbert, William Stout, and others. It also includes three dinosaur sculptures by me, and seven by a brilliant young artist named Stephen Czerkas. But I'm getting ahead of myself. . . .

Back in 1978, when I was just beginning to learn everything I could about dinosaurs, I thought it would be fun to get together with other people who also wanted to learn. By then I had met people who were at the same level of knowledge that I was, and we all formed The Dinosaur Society. Every month we would invite a paleontologist to give a lecture on his or her area of interest. Because we had so many artists in the group, we had great announcements in the tradition of the *Pterodactyl* wings for Waterhouse Hawkins' party. We would have potluck dinner, and discuss our most recent projects. It was a wonderful way to exchange ideas.

All the people in The Dinosaur Society had an interest in paleontology. We had the artists Bil Stout, Mark Hallett, Carl Gage, and Richard Hescox, and the writers George Olshevsky and Don Glut; paleontologists Mark Gallup and George Callison, who runs a program in which people go out and dig up dinosaurs; and preparator Mary Odano, who prepares and casts dinosaur fossils for exhibits after they've been dug up. The Dinosaur Society was successful for about five years, and we all had a wonderful time.

During that period, when I was working with Don Glut on the Charles R. Knight book, we were discussing who we wanted to invite to The Dinosaur Society. Don told me about these two interesting people who made great animated dinosaur films. So I called up Filmation Studios and left a message for Stephen Czerkas and Jim Aupperle. But they weren't in, and somehow the message never got through.

About a year later, I got a call from one of these elusive animators inviting himself to the next meeting. I said, "I know who you are! Come on over!" Stephen got there a bit early, and I liked him immediately. You

Sylvia and Stephen on their wedding day.

see, no one had told me what he looked like or what to expect. What a nice surprise!

We just became better and better friends. Early in our relationship we discussed working together, because we wanted to do similar things. It was a great time of discovery for both of us. Stephen had never worked with paleontologists before, and I was still learning as much as I could about dinosaurs.

One of the things we both wanted to do was to go to Dinosaur National Monument together. About a year after we met, we got married and set off together on our honeymoon to the Dinosaur National Monument and the fossil fields of Alberta, Canada.

Stephen will tell you about the wonderful time we've had since then.

CHAPTER 5

Right from the beginning, Sylvia and I discussed making life-size dinosaurs together. Making a life-size dinosaur is an incredible amount of hard work, so we decided to collaborate. Together we would study and make life-size dinosaurs in our own studio.

This was our dream. And it has all come true.

Of course, I had already made small models for movies. And once I made a fifty-foot sea serpent for a movie called *Monster*. It was a silly looking monster and I'm glad to say it wasn't my design.

But in order to make the most accurate life-size dinosaur models ever, we would have to know absolutely everything possible about dinosaurs. And that meant going to dinosaur sites, talking with all the experts, and reading all the scientific papers. We had to know whatever was available.

On our honeymoon trip to Dinosaur National Monument and in trips we took afterward, we had the opportunity to meet many kind, wonderful people who really helped in our education about dinosaurs. We met Jim Jensen, a world-famous digger of fossils, who has dug up literally tons of dinosaurs over the years. His nickname is "Dinosaur Jim." He has found amazing things, including fossils of the largest dinosaurs ever discovered, *Supersaurus* and *Ultrasaurus*. Phil Currie, one of the main forces behind the Tyrrel Museum of Paleontology in Alberta, Canada, became not only a friend but also a guide who inspired us in our research and studies. So did Dale Russell, another one of the leading paleontologists in North America. They were all generous and helpful and would go out of their way to show us fossil collections and spend time with us. So we were very lucky to receive their help in getting incredible amounts of information very quickly.

The more we learned, traveling around, the more we realized that some of the dinosaur models in museums were inaccurate. What some museums were accepting as impressive simply wasn't. We felt that better-looking and more accurate dinosaurs could be made.

The first attempt I made at something fairly large was a *Tyrannosaurus rex*. I made only the top half of it, at one-quarter its actual size. The skull was about one foot long and quite large, compared to most of my other models. Utilizing my knowledge of special effects, I turned it into a mechanical, cable-controlled puppet so that I could move and manipulate it for films.

Then we started researching the *Allosaurus*, a

fierce meat-eating dinosaur that lived in North America during the Jurassic period. (See the timeline on page 14.) We visited with Jim Madsen, the Utah state paleontologist and expert on the *Allosaurus*. We studied the specimens that had been collected from the Cleveland Loyde quarry in Utah, and looked at *Allosaurus* specimens from museum collections throughout the country. Then we borrowed a cast of the *Allosaurus* skull from the University of California at Berkeley, so that I could make a copy of it and sculpt over it. Jim Madsen also gave us some limb bones he had collected so we could use them in the sculpture. We were ready to start.

We wanted to make a life-size dinosaur. But it had to fit inside our workshop, which at that point was a two-car garage, twenty-five feet across diagonally. It gave us just enough room to do a twenty-two-foot-long *Allosaurus*, which we could squeeze out the door when it was finally completed.

The *Allosaurus* was a test to show what could be done by combining art and science to create truly accurate dinosaurs. Sylvia and I visualize dinosaurs as sleek, elegant, exciting animals, not as big, baggy monsters. They should look like a capable life form. If they are made to look awkward, then they look as if they were a failure of nature, destined to become extinct. In reality, dinosaurs were extremely successful creatures that lived over a span of 155 million years. That's about 150 million years more than humans have lived so far. Certainly dinosaurs were not doomed to extinction because of the way they looked.

That is why accuracy is so important when you're sculpting a dinosaur. I build my sculptures up, as much as possible, from actual casts of the dinosaur bones. I pose the skeleton of the dinosaur in a lifelike position. Then I build the clay muscles directly on the bones, where you can see muscle scars that show where the actual muscles were attached. Muscle scars are little bumps and dips found here and there on the bones. This is where comparing dinosaurs with living creatures is so important. Only by comparing the skeletons of dinosaurs with the skeletons of modern creatures can you tell which forms the muscles should take and how they should be attached to the bones. If the skeletal structure of a dinosaur is similar to that of a living animal, then its muscles were probably similar as well. The hind legs of many dinosaurs resemble the legs of certain birds like chickens and ostriches. Therefore, the muscles and range of movement were probably alike in both shape and behavior.

Also, by studying the living animal you can tell what the muscles will allow the body to do. Of course, you only know how animals move if you observe them for long periods of time. It helps if you live with them and study them daily. That's why Sylvia and I have had dogs and parrots—and two rhinoceros iguanas. Unfortunately, one of our iguanas died after just three years. It was sad, but I tried to make the best of it.

First I made a mold of the animal. Then I had the bones prepared at the museum, so that I had the actual skeleton. Then I could see how the skeleton compared to its body shape. The skeletons have many clues that show what the live animals would look like.

After I've built the clay muscles onto the bones of my sculptures, I apply the clay skin. The outside covering of the animal is most important to the paleoartist, since the skin shows many details of what the dinosaurs looked like.

Dinosaur skin impressions are truly remarkable fossils. It's amazing that anything so fragile could have been preserved for such an incredible length of time. When you find skin impressions, they are very difficult to distinguish from the rock that surrounds the bones. However, you might notice a few scales and then find that the exposed patch could be part of an entire mummified dinosaur.

Dinosaur skin is not made up of flat overlapping scales like the skin of most reptiles that are living today. Instead, dinosaur skin is made of small bumplike scales, called tubercules, that form circular patterns. Some reptiles living today, like the gila monster and the Jackson's chameleon, have similar skin texture.

Dinosaur skin patterns also vary from dinosaur to dinosaur. It is possible to identify different kinds of dinosaurs just by looking at their skin. For example,

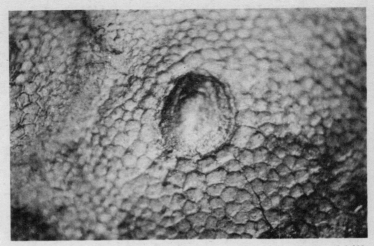

Close-up of fossilized dinosaur skin from a duckbill dinosaur. Collection: National Museum of Natural Sciences, Ottawa, Canada.

the skin of the duckbill dinosaurs looks very different from the skin of horned dinosaurs.

I apply dinosaur skin scale by scale, bump by bump, just the way I did when I was a boy. It's a time-consuming process, but the end result is worth it. When I've finished all of the details, the original clay sculpture is complete and I have a whole dinosaur. Then I'm ready to start making the mold. First, I paint many layers of latex, a kind of rubber, onto the sculpture and then I add cheesecloth to strengthen the latex. The latex mold has to be made in sections. This is because when you're making a mold, each section has to be able to separate easily from the model when it is being cast. Making a mold that won't get stuck on the model is a complicated process.

After the flexible latex mold has been built up, I build layers of rigid fiberglass over it. The fiberglass holds the latex mold in place when it's taken off the clay model.

When the mold is taken off the clay sculpture, the original clay model is often destroyed and set aside. So all you have left is the mold. This is a pretty scary part of the process. But everything is okay as long as the mold has been made properly. Then you make the cast. Liquid resin (which later hardens when mixed with certain chemical compounds), fiberglass, and steel are placed in the sections of the mold, and the mold is reassembled. The mold is closed up. After the resin cast hardens, the mold is opened, and you have a perfect duplicate of the clay model in a permanent material.

It's like making a model kit instead of buying it at the hobby store. The benefit is that you can make as many copies as you desire, instead of having only one clay original. Then the duplicates of the same sculpture become available for different museums.

But it is a very time-consuming process. One thing about the sculptural techniques of molding and casting is that there's no way around them. Today we make the final cast in a synthetic material such as fiberglass. But the basic technique hasn't changed since the time

Building the structure which will support the clay Allosaurus.

of the Greeks, whether the cast is in bronze, silver or gold. (Carving a sculpture, whether from wood, marble, or some other material, is a different process altogether.) The original model is made in oil-based clay, which never hardens. So a mold is necessary to make a permanent copy. Water-based clay, which you bake in a kiln, can only work for smaller models. So if anyone wants be a paleosculptor, they should know how to sculpt, of course, and how to build the metal support system for the heavy clay, and how to make molds and casts.

When I was working on the *Allosaurus,* Sylvia and I could afford enough money for only a few cases of clay at a time. The best oil-based clay is very expensive, and it takes many, many cases of clay to make

Fiberglassing the Allosaurus *body before putting on the clay.*

The completed clay model over which a mold will be made.

Making the latex mold over the clay model.

Removing the mold from the clay model.

The finished product: Stephen's Allosaurus.

a large dinosaur like the *Allosaurus*. So I'd sculpt as much as I could and go back to Hollywood to make some more money to buy clay, and continue on the dinosaur. Because I had to stop so many times, the actual sculpting took far longer than it might have.

Finally, when the model was totally sculpted and I had nearly all the scales on, Sylvia and I went to the Natural History Museum of Los Angeles County to hear the lecture by Dr. José Bonaparte that I described in the introduction. When he told us about finding skin impressions from the meat-eating dinosaur *Carnotaurus,* I was awestruck. The skin on my *Allosaurus* was originally based on the skin of a duckbill, because that was all that was available at the time. But the duckbill was a plant-eating dinosaur. So, when I found out that Dr. Bonaparte had discovered skin impressions from a meat-eating dinosaur, I asked for photographs from him, and then went back and redid the entire skin detail. It was a lot of extra work, but I was happy to find out about the new skin before the *Allosaurus* had been cast. We were very lucky.

CHAPTER 6

Each dinosaur that we work on involves a special challenge. That's because as paleoartists, we have the responsibility of putting scientific knowledge in our sculptures in an artistic way. We can't make fantasy or make-believe dinosaurs. We have to make sculptures that are accurate and pleasing at the same time.

And by doing so, by reading all the scientific literature and going to the quarries and talking to the experts, we usually find that there are suprises in store for us. We often find things about that dinosaur that are both new and exciting for us.

Scientists are working with various new discoveries and ideas. The old picture of the dinosaur as an awkward, sluggish animal has been changed. By looking at fossilized footprints of dinosaurs, scientists can tell how fast the dinosaurs could run. They can tell that dinosaurs didn't have their legs sprawled out to the side, like those of modern reptiles, but held them under their bodies. Their tails didn't drag on the ground, but were held erect. Now we think the dinosaur was sleek, speedy, and, in some cases, might have behaved like many warm-blooded animals living today. All this new information must be in any dinosaur illustration or sculpture.

It is also important to be able to put the dinosaur into its correct environment. For example, if it is a Cretaceous dinosaur (see timeline on page 14), it should be in a setting with other Cretaceous dinosaurs and plants. We know when plants and dinosaurs lived at the same time because their fossilized remains are often found in the same places.

Whenever possible, we try to base our sculptures on actual fossil sites. One of the most famous sites is Egg Mountain, in Montana. Here fossil hunters Dr. John Horner and Robert Makela found nests with dinosaur eggs and the bones of baby hatchlings and nestling dinosaurs. The babies were only about a foot long, but the nestlings were nearly three feet long and were still inside the nest. To John Horner, this meant that these young dinosaurs were being fed and protected by adult dinosaurs. He called the dinosaurs *Maiasaura*, which means "good mother reptile." The idea of dinosaurs looking after their young was very important, because it gave us a new way of understanding what some dinosaur behavior was like.

Sylvia and I visited John's *Maiasaura* nesting sites several times. Because we were already familiar with these baby dinosaurs, the Philadelphia Academy of

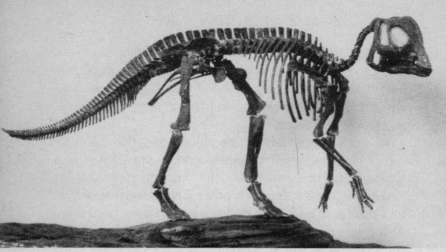

The skeleton of a Maiasaura *nestling by Stephen.*

Sciences asked us to make models of the babies for their new dinosaur exhibit. We discussed the project with Dr. Horner, and he kindly invited us back to make molds of the fossil bones of his nestling *Maiasaura*. Later we cast duplicates of the bones from these molds, and assembled a free-standing skeleton. Many parts of the skeleton were broken or missing, so we reconstructed all of these parts to make the skeleton complete. Then, having made a complete skeleton of the entire nestling dinosaur, we used it as the basis of our clay sculpture. We added the muscles directly over the skeleton, obtaining the natural shape of the little dinosaur. Using fossilized skin impressions of adult dinosaurs, we shrank them down to the proper size of the young nestling dinosaurs. Then, with molds

Maiasaura *nestling life-size sculpture by Stephen.*

of these reduced skin impressions, we covered the clay model with the correct skin texture. We also made models of the foot-long baby *Maiasaura* coming out of the egg, and standing outside of the egg. This project was fun, but it was a great deal of work. And when it was done we were satisfied that we had made our models as accurate as possible.

I've just recently completed a series of sculptures for the California Academy of Sciences, based on another exciting fossil find. In 1964, paleontologist John Ostrom dug up a "brand-new" dinosaur in Montana. This relatively small (ten feet at the most) dinosaur had large, flexible hands and a huge, sharp claw on each of its hind feet. Ostrom named the dinosaur *Deinonychus*, or "terrible claw." It would leap on its prey

Stephen's life-size sculpture of Maiasaura *hatchling.*

and hold onto it with its front hands. Then it would cut and slash with its hind feet. This ferocious little dinosaur might have hunted in packs, and would have moved very quickly indeed.

The Academy wanted to do a large diorama that people could walk around so that it could be seen it from all angles. A diorama is a three-dimensional scene. We wanted to tell the story of a pack of three *Deinonychus* hunting down another dinosaur.

Making the *Deinonychus* diorama, like all of our dinosaur restorations, required much research. We also cooperated with other people who would be working on different aspects of the diorama. Plants had to be researched for accuracy and then specially made.

Working out all of the construction, safety, technical, and artistic details was complicated. But it was also necessary for the exciting and educational dinosaur diorama that we all wanted to see. When the diorama was completed, there would be three ten-foot-long *Deinonychus* chasing after and leaping upon their prey. As people walk around the diorama they would see what it was like when these dinosaurs were hunting. But they would also see what it must have been like to be attacked by these fierce and agile dinosaurs.

After weeks of reconstructing the skull, it was complete and ready to have a mold made of it. At this point we had almost three complete skeletons of *Dei-*

Sylvia and Stephen during the early stages of the Deinonychus *project.*

Stephen in his studio sculpting the Deinonychus *hunting pack.*

nonychus positioned into the desired running poses. These skeletons, now complete with skulls, were somewhat movable. This allowed other designers to change the positions until finally we were all very happy with the postures and final design.

This was challenging, because we wanted to have the three *Deinonychus* positioned differently, even though they were all basically engaged in a similar action. Each became unique in what it was doing and even developed a certain personality. When finished, the three dinosaurs looked totally lifelike. All that was left was to place them in the setting that was waiting for them at the museum. This was a wonderful project to have been involved in. And, like the many other people who helped make it happen, we were proud of a job well done.

The scope and size of the *Deinonychus* project was a little scary at first. But even while we were working on it, we took on another project that was on an even larger scale.

In 1986, while I was giving a lecture in a natural history museum, I was approached by a man named Albert Tsao who seemed to be very interested in dinosaurs. He was very polite and returned to talk with me several times. I was very happy to talk with him, but I thought that he was just an ordinary visitor. To my surprise, Mr. Tsao explained that he was looking for someone to be in charge of a new dinosaur hall that was going to be built in Taipei, Taiwan. A major part of the museum was going to be a gigantic, full-scale, walk-through diorama depicting many different types of dinosaurs. These included many of the largest and most popular dinosaurs, like *Tyrannosaurus rex, Triceratops, Apatosaurus* and *Stegosaurus*. Mr. Tsao asked if I would be willing to come to Taiwan and be in charge of constructing the dinosaurs for the new museum. I was a bit overwhelmed at the size of the project, but very tempted. I explained that I would only want to become involved if the museum could give me its assurance that the models would be the best and most accurate ones ever built. Mr. Tsao told me that they would make sure of that.

The next step was for the museum to send me the blueprints and drawings of the dinosaurs that they wanted made. This way, I could make corrections before we actually visited Taiwan. When I received the drawings of the dinosaurs I was impressed. But just as I feared, the realism of the drawings couldn't hide the fact that the artists' image of the dinosaurs was inaccurate and oversized. My job began immediately. I made an entire set of new drawings following their guidelines, but making corrections where necessary. After I returned my new drawings to Taiwan, their artists made scale models from my drawings. When these were completed in clay, Sylvia and I made our first trip to Taipei to correct the scale models. Later, during our second trip, we coordinated the building of the full-size models.

Stephen and a huge life-size model of of a Tyranno-saurus rex *at the museum in Taipei, Taiwan.*

Then on our third and final trip, Sylvia and I demonstrated how to paint the dinosaurs, completing the *Tyrannosaurus rex, Triceratops* and *Stegosaurus.* We made our choice of colors by comparing colors and patterns of animals that are living today and used them as a guide for making the dinosaurs as natural looking as possible. For example, a small meat-eating dinosaur could have a camouflage pattern in shades of brown and gray. We also worked with the artists who were reconstructing the plants, and with the artists who were painting the background mural that would blend in with the sculptures. This was an exciting part of the project. With the painted background we could add more information about the actual world that the dinosaurs lived in. We could show the landscape and plants and we could add more dinosaurs as well. The additional animals included in the background mural made a more complete story of what the dinosaurs were really like. For instance, we had a sculpted *Tyrannosaurus rex* and *Triceratops* confronting each other. But we wanted to show that there was more to their lives than just eating and fighting. So in the mural we decided to have a baby *Triceratops* running back to a large herd that was grazing in the distance. We hoped to imply not only that herding dinosaurs stayed together for safety, but also that there might have been a caring side to some dinosaurs and that they may even have looked after and protected their young.

With the *Apatosaurus*, we felt that it was important to show that it was able to do many different kinds of things. The *Apatosaurus* has almost always been shown standing still in the water, ferns dripping from its mouth. We showed the *Apatosaurus* in various locations: happily swimming about in the water and eating, but also walking on the dry land into the forests.

When the background murals had been completed and the plants and scenery finally surrounded the finished models, the museum had an entire walk-through diorama of the Dinosaur Era. Ten life-size beasts ranging from ten to eighty feet long stood in the completed dinosaur hall.

Included among the life-size dinosaurs in the Taipei museum was one for which I had a special fondness and certain kind of pride. It was the *Stegosaurus*. What was unique about the model was that it used my new discovery about how the armored plates were positioned along the animal's back.

At first glance, this *Stegosaurus* may not look very different from other reconstructions of this popular dinosaur. I had made a small but important change. I had discovered that the armored plates that were along the top of the animal were arranged in a single row, and not in two rows as most everyone had believed. People have often disagreed on how the two rows of armored plates were arranged on the *Stegosaurus*. Even as a child, I remember discussing this problem with my friends at school. Like everyone else, I simply accepted the idea that the armored plates of the *Stegosaurus* were in two rows. But how were they arranged—in pairs, or alternating? This was the question that I wanted to solve.

Interpreting fossils, especially the fossils of dinosaurs, is often difficult. But scientists have to work with what fossil evidence exists and do the best they can. When I first began to work on the *Stegosaurus,* I studied all the fossil discoveries. Once I was reading through a stack of scientific papers when suddenly a strange new idea came to mind. I turned to Sylvia and said, 'You know, I'm not so sure that the plates are even in two rows to begin with." I had stumbled on to a new line of thinking. I continued searching through the papers, and letters and came across an old manuscript that was all about *Stegosaurus*. It was scientific study that was never completed or published. It was written by an important paleontologist, Dr. F. A. Lucas, in 1901. He was restudying *Stegosaurus* fossils that had been already studied by an earlier paleontologist, Professor O. C. Marsh.

While at the Smithsonian Museum, I had the chance to examine the same *Stegosaurus* fossils that had been studied by Dr. Lucas and Professor Marsh. One in particular was of great importance. It has the distinction of still being the most complete *Stegosaurus* ever discovered, even though it was found over a hundred years ago, in 1886 and 1887. I noticed that only the upper parts of some plates overlapped. Curiously, the bottom parts that would have been embedded into the skin of the animal *never* overlapped. This became more and more exciting as I continued to think about what I saw. I thought of a simple test that would tell me if I was on the right track, that the plates should be arranged in a single row. From my measurements I recreated the total length of the *Stegosaurus*. Then using the total of the combined lengths of all of the plates of this specimen, I could compare the two measurements and see if it was at all possible for the plates to be in a single row. Much to my surprise, I found out that all seventeen plates could easily fit along the length of the animal in one single row. I realized that this specimen was even more complete than had been thought, and that no plates were missing.

Stephen's skeletal drawing demonstrates that all of the Stegosaurus's *plates can fit in a single row.*

I wrote a technical paper explaining my conclusions about the *Stegosaurus*. Soon thereafter, word of my new idea began to reach the news media. I was approached by many reporters who wanted to write articles about it. It was very gratifying to be accepted not only by scientists, but by the dinosaur fans as well. Working on the problem of the *Stegosaurus* plates was an exciting detective project. I was fortunate to have solved one of the mysteries about dinosaurs. But the science of paleontology, including the study of dinosaurs, builds upon new discoveries and interpretations. These discoveries continue to give us a better understanding of the dinosaurs.

I gave a talk on my new discovery at the opening of the "Dinosaurs Past and Present" exhibit Sylvia put together. Sylvia has already told you what a great

The *"new"* Stegasaurus *by Stephen.*

success that exhibit was. The public was so enthusiastic that attendence records were often set for many of the museums on the exhibition tour.

I occasionally give lectures while visiting museums in different cities. It's always fun to explain things about dinosaurs and hear what kinds of questions people ask. Recently, I gave a week-long demonstration at the Royal Ontario Museum of Natural History in Toronto, Canada. There I showed how I restore the living form of a dinosaur from its fossils. I restored the face of a dinosaur on one side of its skull, while leaving the opposite side untouched for a comparison.

Working directly over a cast model of an *Albertosaurus* skull, I began by adding modeling clay to where the muscles of the jaw would have been attached in real life. For the first three days, I continued to build up the shape of the head by forming the muscles over the bone. While answering many questions, I explained that by first restoring the muscles I could make the reconstruction more accurate. Being familiar with the anatomy of living animals, I could make comparisons that I could use as a guide. Then I placed a realistic looking eye that I had made out of plastic into the opening where it belonged in the skull. This began to really bring a sense of life to the dinosaur's face.

For the next few days I added the skin details directly over the muscles. By pressing the clay into special molds that I had made from fossilized dinosaur skin, I was able to make patches of thin sheets of clay that had the actual scales of real dinosaur skin on them. Then I took the patches of "skin" and covered the head muscles with them. After carefully applying this skin, I stamped on more scales wherever they were needed.

It was a complicated process. But it was rewarding to see the reactions of people as they became aware of what I had to do in order to make the face of this dinosaur. They were fascinated to see that by using science it was possible to see what a dinosaur really should look like. Many people even returned to see the later stages as I restored the face of the *Albertosaurus*. It was a busy week, but I was happy to show that it is possible to accurately recreate dinosaurs, and that education was much more helpful than just relying on imagination.

Stephen sculpting the face of an Albertosaurus *at the Royal Ontario Museum in Toronto, Canada.*

CHAPTER 7

One of the most enjoyable parts of Sylvia's and my work is digging for dinosaur fossils. This is always exciting. Of course, there is a great deal of hard work. But it's all worth it when we find the fossils that we're looking for. Its incredible to think that as we carefully and slowly remove the fossil bones from the surrounding rock, we are the first people to ever see the remains of these dinosaurs that have been hidden in the earth for millions of years. And the sunlight that shines down on them is the first light that has touched these fossils since the dinosaurs were alive, over 65 million years ago!

You might think that digging dinosaur fossils from the ground must be tiring and difficult. And in fact it *can* be quite difficult. But the feeling of satisfaction more than makes up for the hardships that are involved.

Every year during the summer months, when the weather is warm, or even incredibly hot, Sylvia and

Sylvia with a Pachyrhinosaurus *horn boss that was found on a dig in Alberta, Canada.*

I go out in the field looking for fossils. This involves camping and hiking through rather desolate areas that are known as the badlands. They are called badlands because they are usually desertlike. They're too harsh for people, and not even many plants can live there. But for paleontologists like us, the *badlands* are actually the *best lands* for finding fossils. Many of the existing badlands are undeveloped and mostly untouched. This has allowed the fossils to remain protected, while the process of erosion brings them closer to the surface, where they can be found. In North America, the best places for finding fossils are the badlands of Montana, Utah, Wyoming, the Dakotas, and Alberta, Canada.

Fossils can be found in many places other than the badlands. It's rare, but occasionally at construction sites or road cuts tractors will uncover the fossil bones of long-extinct animals. Even farmers plowing their fields have found that what may at first have looked like a cow bone is actually a fossil bone. Fossils can be found in almost any part of the world, but the erosion that is so active in the badlands brings the fossils to the surface and increases the chance of finding them.

You have to be lucky to find fossils, but you must also be persistent and knowledgeable about what you are hoping to find. It is almost impossible to find something if you don't know what to look for. That's why before anyone goes looking for fossils, they should first study and learn as much about the fossils as they can. As with anything in life, being prepared will make your work easier and more rewarding.

Sylvia and I had studied a great deal and knew a lot about dinosaurs and fossils before we went on our first digs. On several of our first digs we were both assistants, helping other paleontologists who were in charge. It was important to learn the tricks of the trade from these experienced people. They taught us a great deal that could not be learned in a classroom, but only from first-hand experience.

Over the years, I have developed something of a knack for finding fossils. Where often people would simply walk past a rock I would stop, fall to my knees and say "Back here! I've found something." Their response would often be, "But how did you spot that? We certainly didn't see it." It all comes to a little luck. But, more importantly, it takes being prepared and knowing what to look for.

When a fossil is first discovered it may still be mostly covered and hidden in the ground. This is actually better than finding all of the fossil totally uncovered, because the fossils are usually fragile and would be easily destroyed if they were exposed to the weather for very long. When searching for fossils, the luck involved is mostly in finding them at the proper time, just as they first appear, and not after they are destroyed by erosion. Once a fossil has been found it is carefully dug around, separated from the earth, and exposed. Special glues and protective hardeners are applied to the fossil, so that all of the broken parts remain intact. This is a slow process that requires a great deal of patience and skill.

The surrounding rock can often have the same color and texture as a fossil, and hide where different parts of it are located. This is why you have to be extremely careful when digging up fossils. Hidden parts can be

Stephen digging for dinosaur fossils in Utah.

destroyed and lost forever. When starting to uncover a fossil bone, it becomes important to identify which bone you are working on and how it is positioned. As soon as you know which bone it is, the rest of the removal process becomes easier and safer.

Often, the one bone that you are working on is mixed together with many other bones all around it. Sorting them out can become very complicated. Of course, the more fossil bones the better, and one simply has to take the time to dig them out properly. This often requires days, and in some cases even weeks. First the fossil bones are carefully uncovered, hardened with glues and dug all around. Then their positions are recorded and mapped for later studies. All of the fossil bones are then covered with paper or aluminum foil, followed by layers of plaster and burlap. The paper and aluminum foil act as a barrier to prevent the plaster from sticking to and harming the fossil when the plaster jacket is finally removed. After the plaster becomes hard, the fossil can be safely flipped over and removed from the ground. The plaster and burlap act as a protective jacket, in which the fossil can be carried back to the museum. There the plaster jackets are opened and the fossil bones cleaned and repaired as necessary.

I remember one difficult and challenging dig in particular. Sylvia and I were helping a Montana high school get a skull of a *Triceratops* for an educational display. Ranchers had found this skull, perched some fifty feet up the side of a hill, just overhanging the edge of the cliff. The skull was huge, remarkably complete, and in one piece. It was positioned upright and was facing outward, as if looking beyond to the horizon. Nearly eight feet in length, it must have weighed well over a ton.

The problem of digging it out was made even tougher by its location, high up on the cliff. Before we started digging around the skull, we explored the bottom of the cliff to see if we could find the horns. They had been exposed to erosion, which had caused them to break off and fall down the cliff. Fortunately, we found that most of the broken horns were still

This Triceratops *skull is very much like the one rescued from the cliff in Montana.*

intact and could be reattached to the skull later, when it was being prepared for display. But first, there was an incredible amount of hard digging that was necessary to safely remove the skull from the cliff. Paths had to be dug and cut before we could even reach the skull and work around it. We were lucky to have several high school students to help do the heavy digging.

In a few days, the skull was all dug around and ready for the plaster jackets to be applied. This can be a real messy part of the job. Somehow, I usually get to do it. The skull was entirely undercut, and was supported on only two short pillars of rock that remained underneath it. I covered the top and sides of the skull with plaster and burlap. Then I had to crawl underneath it and stick more plaster and burlap on the exposed bottom parts before trying to move it. This was dangerous and difficult. There was at least a ton of rock hanging out over me, and I had so little space to work in that I actually scraped my nose as I turned my head from side to side.

When I had finished putting on the plaster, I crawled out from under the skull as fast as I could. Later we built a wooden sled around the skull, so that we could pull it across the hill to where it could be placed on a truck and driven away. We attached steel cables to

Triceratops *sculpted by Stephen and Sylvia together.*

the wooden sled and to the back of the truck. We thought our job would be finished soon and the skull would be on its way back to the high school.

Much to our amazement, when the truck started to pull the sled that was carrying the skull, something went wrong. The skull didn't move. Instead, the truck reeled up the cables and was pulled backward toward the skull! Instantly, the driver of the truck stopped. The skull was just too big and heavy, and what we needed was a much bigger truck. The ranchers decided to go into the nearest town, which was almost a hundred miles away. There they would rent an oversized tow-truck that was capable of hauling large vehicles, like buses or tractors. It took most of the day for them to return with the tow-truck. But when they hooked up the steel cables, the sled and skull were slowly, yet easily pulled into place on the back of the truck. Having the proper tools, in this case a huge tow-truck, certainly made our work easier. We were all pleased to see the skull safely on its way.

As we have become more experienced over the years, Sylvia and I have been in charge of fossil digs of our own. Together we have dug up many dinosaur fossils that have become parts of the collections of museums. We have collected different types of dinosaurs, including the armor-plated *Stegosaurus*, the gigantic long-necked sauropods, like the *Apatosaurus*, the multi-horned *Triceratops*, duck-billed *hadrosaurs*, and even a *Tyrannosaurus rex*. We have also found nests of dinosaur eggs and fossilized skin impressions. It has always been fun digging for dinosaurs. We look forward to when we can return to the badlands, where we hope to find more fossil bones, and maybe even a new type of dinosaur that's never been seen before.

CHAPTER 8

Sylvia and I have always been fortunate in having strong interests and being able to develop them. Since the age of four, I have known what I want to do with my life. And although it has gone in many directions, I have always worked toward goals that would make me the happiest—and, I hope, a better person. Sharing my interests with Sylvia has increased all of the happiness in my life. We are lucky to have each day together, in which we can learn, work, and enjoy the world around us.

Our fascination with dinosaurs has taken us to many distant and different parts of the world. One of the nicest things is having the opportunity to meet other people who are also interested in learning more about dinosaurs and life of the past. Developing a working relationship and friendship with others is one of the rewards of paleontology.

During the past few years, we have created a studio in which we construct life-size models of dinosaurs for museums. It is located in a building so big that we can make even the largest of dinosaurs. And that is exactly what we hope to continue to do for years to come. We have already completed several smaller dinosaur models, including the ten-foot-long *Deinonychus*, and a twenty-foot-long prehistoric sea-going reptile called *Mosasaurus.* We are currently working on a life-size model of the *Carnotaurus,* which will be over thirty feet long. It's always exciting to see dinosaurs as large as they would have been when they were alive. Our studio is also a place where we can continue our research and studies.

When Sylvia and I entered the field of paleontology and the study of dinosaurs, we already had specific artistic talents and interests. In a real sense we even created our own place in paleontology by persistently showing what we could do. It's required a great deal of hard work and dedication, but it's all been worth it. In fact, it's been a lot of fun.

Many people might think of paleontologists as having dull jobs, tediously working with dirty, dusty bones. But, in so many ways, paleontology is an exciting and fulfilling profession. It's like being an astronaut searching for life on other planets. Rather than looking somewhere in space, paleontologists look somewhere in time. Discovering the fossil remains of ancient life is as awesome and thrilling as anything that can be imagined.

If you want to become a paleontologist, there are

Sylvia sculpting a Tyrannosaurus rex.

many different opportunities to choose from. You can be a field worker, someone who goes out and actually digs up fossils. This is a perfect job for someone who loves camping and the great outdoors. Museums and universities also need many kinds of dinosaur experts. You can be a preparator, the person who works in the lab and prepares the bones. The preparator cleans and mends the bones after they have been dug up. You can be the scientist who analyzes fossils, or the teacher who teaches others about them. You can be a curator, as Sylvia is, and present information to the public in a museum exhibit. You can be a writer, and write about dinosaurs, or you can be a painter or a sculptor.

Stephen posing with Apatosaurus *and* Tyrannosaurus rex *animation models.*

For young people who are interested in dinosaurs, there are lots of ways to learn about them. First, you can read books. We've included a list of good books on dinosaurs at the back of this volume, but these are only a small percentage of what's actually available. Then, you can go to your local dinosaur or natural history museum. Many have classes that you can take to learn about dinosaurs. If no museum is close enough to get to regularly, you might be able to visit it on school trips or with your parents. Today, there are dinosaur exhibits all across North America and throughout the world. You might be able to find one close to you in the list of dinosaur museums at the back of this book.

Like other sciences, paleontology seeks to discover and understand the unknown. There are always new dinosaurs waiting to be dug up, and new things about them to learn. Sylvia and I are happy to be part of a worldwide team of scientists, artists, and writers making these discoveries every day. We invite you to join us.

Sylvia and Stephen with the leg from Jim Jensen's Ul-trasaurus, *one of the largest dinosaurs ever discovered.*

102

Dinosaur Museums

United States

1. Academy of Natural Sciences
   Philadelphia, Pennsylvania
2. American Museum of Natural History
   New York, New York
3. Carnegie Museum of Natural History
   Pittsburg, Pennsylvania
4. Denver Museum of Natural History
   Denver, Colorado
5. Dinosaur National Monument
   Jensen, Utah
6. Earth Sciences Museum
   Brigham Young University, Provo, Utah
7. Field Museum of Natural History
   Chicago, Illinois
8. Houston Museum of Natural Sciences
   Houston, Texas
9. Los Angeles County Museum of Natural History
   Los Angeles, California
10. Museum of Comparative Zoology
    Harvard University, Cambridge, Massachusetts
11. Museum of Paleontology
    University of California, Berkeley, California
12. Museum of the Rockies
    Montana State University, Bozeman, Montana
13. National Museum of Natural History
    Smithsonian Institution, Washington, DC

14. Nebraska State Museum
    Nebraska University, Lincoln, Nebraska
15. Peabody Museum of Natural History
    Yale University, New Haven, Connecticut
16. Science Museum of St. Paul
    St. Paul, Minnesota
17. Texan Memorial Museum
    University of Texas, Austin, Texas
18. University of Wyoming Geological Museum
    Laramie, Wyoming
19. Utah Museum of Natural History
    University of Utah, Salt Lake City, Utah
20. Cleveland Museum of Natural History
    Cleveland, Ohio

Canada

21. Dinosaur Provincial Park
    Patricia, Alberta
22. National Museum of Natural Sciences
    Ottawa, Ontario
23. Tyrell Museum of Paleontology
    Drumheller, Alberta
24. Royal Ontario Museum
    Toronto, Ontario

Bibliography

Benton, Michael. *The Dinosaur Encyclopedia*. Illustrated by Wendy Barish. Wanderer/Simon & Schuster, 1984.

Bischoff, David. *Search for Dinosaurs*. Illustrated by Doug Henderson and Alex Nino. Bantam Books, 1984.

Butterworth, Oliver. *The Enormous Egg*. Illustrated by Louis Darling. Atlantic: Little, 1956; Dell, 1978.

Cohen, Daniel. *Dinosaurs*. Illustrated by Jean Zallinger. Doubleday, 1987.

Colbert, Edwin H. *Dinosaurs: An Illustrated History*. Hammond Inc., 1983.

*Czerkas, Sylvia and Donald Glut. *Dinosaurs, Mammoths, and Cavemen—The Art of Charles R. Knight*. E.P. Dutton, 1982.

*Czerkas, Sylvia and Everett Olson, Editors. *Dinosaurs Past and Present Symposium Volumes I and II*. Natural History Museum of Los Angeles County and the University of Washington Press, 1987.

Glut, Donald. *The Dinosaur Dictionary*. Citadel Press, 1976.

Horner, John and James Gorman. *Maia: A Dinosaur Grows Up*. Illustrated by Doug Henderson. Running Press, 1987.

*Horner, John and James Gorman. *Digging Dinosaurs*. Workman, 1988.

Lauber, Patricia. *Dinosaurs Walked Here and Other Stories Fossils Tell*. Bradbury, 1986.

Lerangis, Peter. *Last of the Dinosaurs*. Illustrated by Doug Henderson. Bantam Books, 1988.

Mannetti, William. *Dinosaurs in Your Backyard*. Illustrated by the author. Atheneum, 1982.

Norman, David. *The Illustrated Encyclopedia of Dinosaurs*. Illustrated by John Sibbick. Crescent Books/Crown, 1985.

*Russell, Dale A. *A Vanished World: The Dinosaurs of Western Canada*. National Museum of Natural Sciences, 1977.

Sattler, Helen. *Baby Dinosaurs*. Illustrated by Jean Day Zallinger. Lothrop, Lee & Shepard, 1984.

*Service, William. Byron Preiss, Editor. *The Dinosaurs*. Illustrated by William Stout. Bantam Books, 1981.

*Willford, John. *The Riddle of the Dinosaur*. Knopf, 1985.

Zallinger, Peter. *Dinosaurs and Other Archosaurs*. Illustrated by the author. Random House, 1986.

*Books for older readers.

About the Authors

Stephen Czerkas was born in Alhambra, California. As a sculptor and paleontologist his specialty is life-size dinosaur models for museum exhibits. His lifelong interest in dinosaurs started at the age of four when he sculpted his first dinosaur. He continued making dinosaurs and other animation models for movies as a special effects artist from 1970 to 1981. Since 1981 he has received commissions for life-size dinosaurs from the Natural History Museum of Los Angeles, the California Academy of Sciences, The New Mexico Museum of Natural History, and the Philadelphia Academy of Sciences. His dinosaurs are also on display at the Tyrrell Museum of Palaeontology, Alberta, the Museum of the Rockies, Montana, and elsewhere. Currently he and Sylvia are writing a dinosaur book.

Sylvia Czerkas was born in Detroit, Michigan. She graduated from California State University, Los Angeles. From 1968 to 1982 she worked as a fine artist exhibiting her sculptures in art galleries and museums. Her sculptures were of modern animals, as well as endangered or extinct species, including the dinosaurs. In 1981 she co-authored *Dinosaurs, Mammoths, and Cavemen—the Art of Charles R. Knight* and assembled a traveling museum exhibit of Knight's artworks. As guest curator for the Natural History

Museum of Los Angeles she organized the "Dinosaurs Past and Present" exhibition which is currently traveling throughout North America and the United Kingdom, and was the co-author of the exhibit's symposium and catalogue volumes. She assists her husband, Stephen, in the management of their sculpture studio, and together they spend their summers digging for dinosaurs.